Is Everyone Ready for FUN?

For Andrew

 • ISBN 978-0-545-53375-1 •
 • Published by Scholastic Inc., 557 Broadway, New York, NY 10012, by arrangement with Simon & Schuster Books for Young Readers, an imprint of Simon & Schuster Children's Publishing Division. • 12 11 10 9 8 7 6 5 4 13 14 15 16 17 18/0 • Printed in the U.S.A. 40 • First Scholastic printing, January 2013 • The text for this book is set in Chaloops. • The illustrations for this book are rendered digitally.

Look! It's
Chicken's
sofa!

PLOP

Is Everyone Ready for FUN?

by Jan Thomas

SCHOLASTIC INC.

It's time to . . .

JUMP!

Up and down,
up and down.

Let's all
JUMP
up and down!

On Chicken's sofa!

Wait a minute!
There's no
JUMPING
on my sofa!

Oh. Okay, Chicken.
We won't JUMP on your sofa anymore.

Is EVERYONE ready for MORE FUN?!

MORE FUN?!

It's time to . . .

DANCE!
Back and forth,
back and forth.

Let's all
DANCE
back and forth!

On Chicken's sofa!

WHAT
are you
doing now?!

You said not to JUMP on your sofa.
We weren't JUMPING.

Is EVERYONE ready for EVEN MORE FUN?!

NO MORE FUN!!

It's time to . . .

WIGGLE!

To and fro,
to and fro.

Let's all
WIGGLE
to and fro!

On Chicken's sofa!

ENOUGH!

There will be no more
JUMPING, DANCING,
or **WIGGLING**
on my sofa!!

Then there's only one thing left for us to do. . . .

Is EVERYONE ready?

It's time to . . .

NAP!

NAPPING
on my sofa?

yes.

Good idea!